This book is for my children, Jeremy and Andrea,
who have always been my biggest fans.
Thank you for believing in my creativity!

www.mascotbooks.com

For more information, please contact:
Mascot Books
620 Herndon Parkway #320
Herndon, VA 20170
info@mascotbooks.com

Library of Congress Control Number: 2018910879

CPSIA Code: PRT1018A
ISBN-13: 978-1-68401-898-7

Printed in the United States

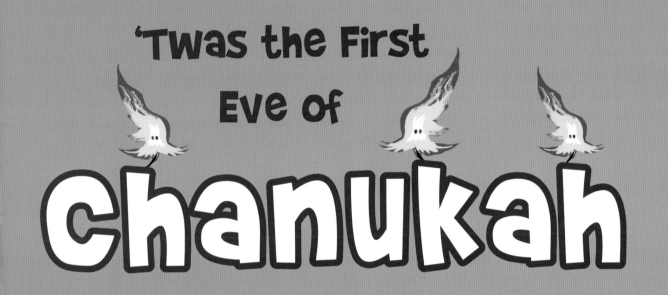

'Twas the First Eve of Chanukah

Dayna J. Zimmerman

illustrated by Alejandro Echavez

'Twas the First Eve of Chanukah and all through my home
Not a single person was moving about—not even cousin Jerome.

The candles were lit on the table with care,
In anticipation that Chanukah Harry soon would be there.

The children were tucked and asleep in their beds,
While visions of dreidels danced in their heads.

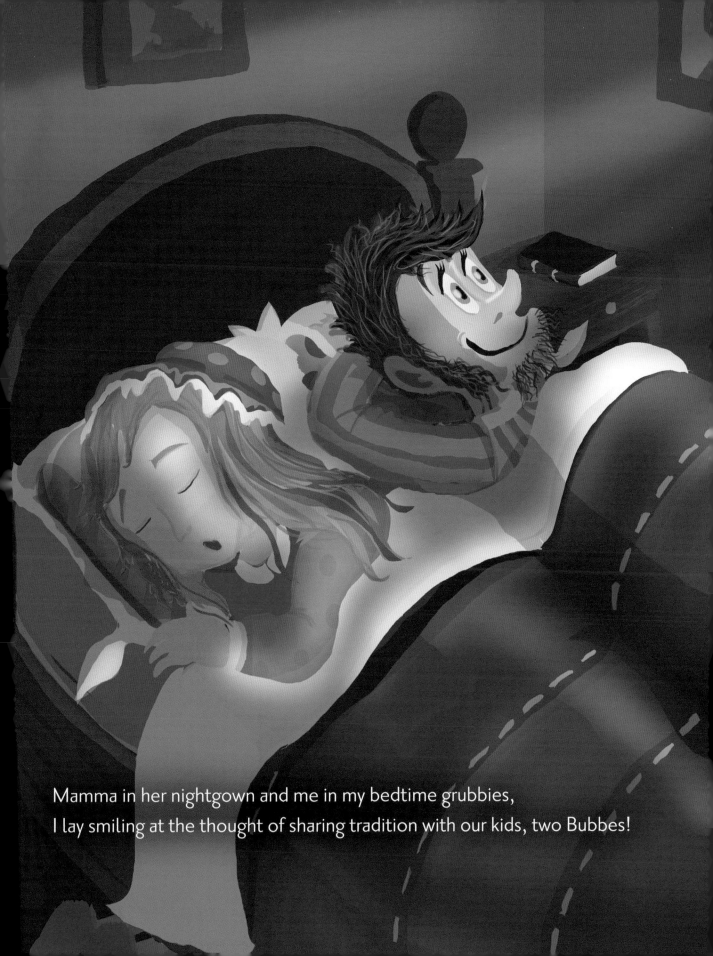

Mamma in her nightgown and me in my bedtime grubbies,
I lay smiling at the thought of sharing tradition with our kids, two Bubbes!

When out on the lawn, I saw a bright light,
I flew from my bed to see such a sight.

Away to the window, I ran in a flutter,
Threw open the curtains and even the shutter.

The light from the object on the new fallen snow,
Gave a feeling of noontime on everything below.

When what should I see through the holes of the door handle,
But a big giant shamus and eight little candles.

With a sweet little man, I should love my girl to marry,
I knew on the spot that it must be Chanukah Harry.

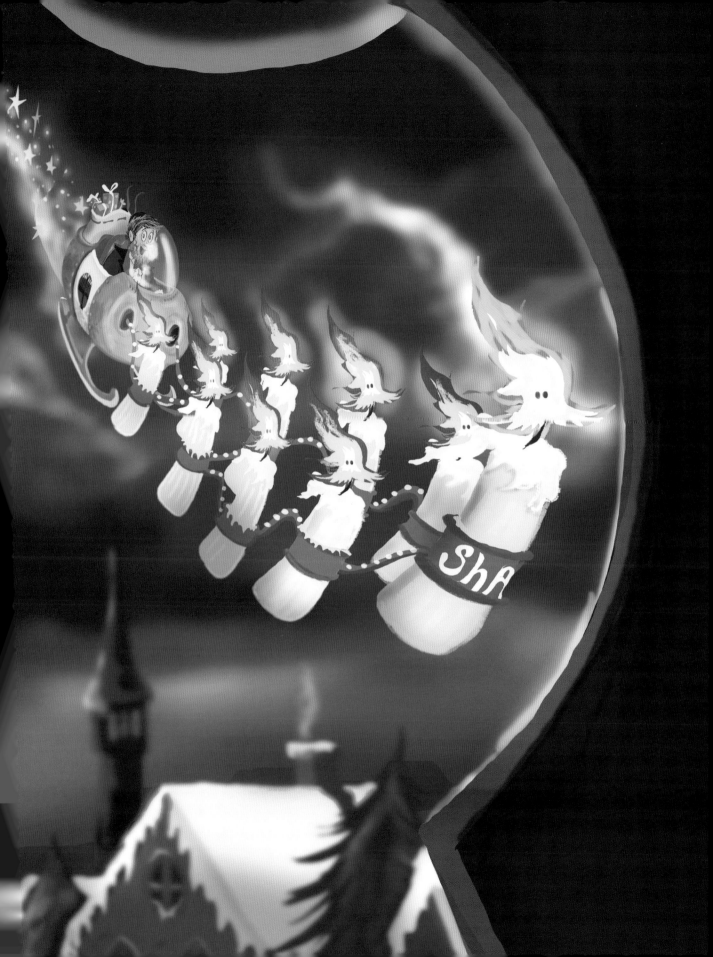

Much faster than eagles, his candles they came,
And he hummed and he sang and he called them by name:

"Now Moses, now Abraham, now Cain and Abel,
On Jonathan, on Noah, on Isaac and Mabel!"

To the top of the minivan, to the house at the back,
Now, flicker about, flicker about, flicker about, you big pack.

Then up to the housetop the candles they flew,
With a menorah full of goodies, and Chanukah Harry, too.

Up above, I heard pretty quick,
The spitter and spatter of eight tiny wicks.

As I peeked in my head and was turning about,
Down the chimney Chanukah Harry came with a shout.

He was dressed in blue velvet from his head to his foot,
But his clothes were all tarnished with dry leaves and some soot.

A bundle of goodies he had taken from his back,
He looked like a robber with a big swollen sack.

His eyes how they twinkled. He had no dimples.
His cheeks were like cherries. His nose like a pickle!

His cute little mouth resembled the bottom tip of a dreidel,
And his chin was in the shape of a chicken soup ladle.

The end of his pipe he held tight in his teeth,
And the smoke encircled him as it gave off a little heat.

He had a pudgy little face and a stomach like a swollen river
That shook when he laughed like a bowl of chopped liver.

He was short and stout and resembled a North Pole Elf,
But I had to laugh when I saw him, because he looked like myself.

The flick of his light and the tilt of his head
Soon let me know he wanted me to go back to bed.

He spoke not a word, something I had not expected of him.
But instead filled the dreidels, then turned with a spin.

He looked up the chimney and said, "No More!
Next year I start by coming in the front door."

He jumped into his menorah and clapped his hands twice,
And away they all flew into the dead of the night.

But some Yiddish he exclaimed as he drove out of sight.
He said, "Happy Chanukah to all and to all a good night!"

ABout the Author

Originally from Boston, Dayna Zimmerman is a graduate of Syracuse University. She currently resides in the Midwest with her two college-aged children. In her spare time, Dayna enjoys creative writing.

Loving the holiday season, Dayna always looks forward to decorating and celebrating the traditions of Chanukah with her family and friends. When her children were younger, she came up with the character of Chanukah Harry who became a substitute icon for Santa Claus to symbolize the holiday for her kids.

'Twas the First Eve of Chanukah is Dayna's first children's book.